UNIV. OF MOUNT UNION
CURRICULUM CENTER

Abby's Chairs

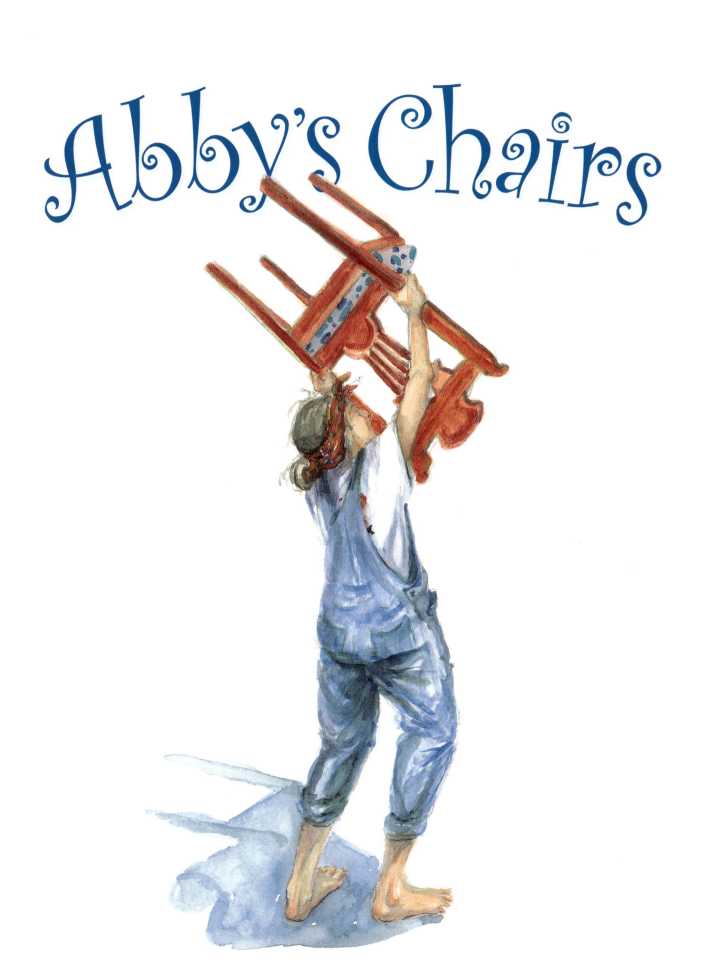

For Michael, Laura, Beth, Chad,
and Maryann
—*B. S.*

With all my love, to my "relatively" patient brood:
Beluga, Ms. B, Opal, and Emilia
—*D. S.*

Text ©2004 Barbara Santucci
Illustrations © 2004 Debrah Santini

Published 2004 by Eerdmans Books for Young Readers
An imprint of Wm. B. Eerdmans Publishing Company
255 Jefferson S.E., Grand Rapids, Michigan 49503
P.O. Box 163, Cambridge CB3 9PU U.K.

All rights reserved
Printed in China

04 05 06 07 08 09 10 7 6 5 4 3 2 1

Library of Congress Cataloging-in-Publication Data
Santucci, Barbara.
Abby's chairs / written by Barbara Santucci ; illustrated by Debrah Santini.
p. cm.
Summary: No matter what changes she makes, Abby's old chairs just don't look right
in her new home until some friendly townspeople show her the value of a fresh perspective.

ISBN 0-8028-5205-X (alk. paper)

[1. Chairs-Fiction. 2. Interior decoration-Fiction. 3. Friendship-Fiction.] I. Santini, Debrah, ill. II. Title.
PZ7.S23863 Ab 2004
[E]—dc21
2002151768

The illustrations were rendered in watercolor.
The display type was set in Hoefler Regular and Curlz.
The text type was set in Hoefler Regular.
Art Director Gayle Brown
Graphic Design Matthew Van Zomeren

Abby's Chairs

Written by Barbara Santucci · Illustrated by Debrah Santini

Eerdmans Books for Young Readers
Grand Rapids, Michigan • Cambridge, U.K.

Abby loved her new home. She loved to sniff the violets blooming in her sunroom. She loved to soak in bubbled bath water in her footed, purple tub. She loved to see the sun rising outside her bedroom window.

But there was one thing Abby didn't love. She didn't love how her chairs looked in her new home.

"How can that be?" she wondered. "My chairs always looked wonderful in my old house. Maybe they need a fresh coat of paint."

So Abby headed to the hardware store where she piled cans of paint into her shopping cart: red and green and tangerine, purple and yellow and aquamarine. She wheeled them to the checkout counter.

"Welcome to Harold's Hardware," said the clerk. "I'm Harold."

"I'm Abby, and I live in the yellow house on Fern Road. Stop by anytime."

"Why, thank you," said Harold, handing Abby her change.

Abby picked up her shopping bags and walked home.

All that day and the next day too, Abby sanded
and smoothed, painted and polished. And when she
was done, each chair shouted its own color.

But when she lined
them up, they still didn't
look right.

"My chairs always looked
wonderful in my old house,"
Abby sighed. "Maybe they
need some new fabric."

So she headed for the fabric
store where she selected stripes
and spots, checks and dots. She
piled them onto the counter.

"What lovely fabric you've
chosen," said the clerk. "My name
is Betsy."

"I'm Abby, and I'm sewing new
chair cushions. I live in the yellow
house on Fern Road. Stop by
anytime."

"Why, thank you," said Betsy,
handing her a coupon. "Save this
for your next visit to our store."

Abby picked up her bundles
and walked home.

All that day and
the next day too,
Abby snipped and
stitched, adding
buttons and lace.

And when she was done, each chair sang its own personality. But when she looked at them, they still didn't look right.

"My chairs always looked wonderful in my old house," Abby sniffed. "Maybe they need to be arranged differently."

So Abby headed for the library where she sorted and searched, pored and perched, looking for books with exciting decorating tips. She found the perfect book: *How to Arrange Your Chairs in Your New Home.*

The librarian said, "You must be new in town."

"Yes, I am. I'm Abby, and I live in the yellow house on Fern Road. Stop by anytime."

"Well, thank you. My name is Grace. Enjoy your book."

Abby picked up her book and walked home.

All that day, and the next
day, too, Abby arranged her
chairs in circles and squares,
by lamps and by stairs.

She hung them on hooks, from ceiling and walls. She pushed them and pulled them from hall to hall. She set them in the tub and sadly shrugged, because they still did not look right.

Finally, Abby collapsed into one of her chairs and sighed, "My chairs always looked wonderful in my old house. What more can I do?" Abby thought for a long while. "Maybe I just have too many chairs."

So she carried them, one
by one, out onto the lawn.
Abby made a sign: FREE
CHAIRS.

Then she sat in the shade
and gazed sadly at her
chairs.

Before long, Harold
from the hardware store
stopped by.

"Thought you could use some brush cleaner." He glanced at the chairs. "My, you've been busy." He brought one into the shade and sat beside Abby. The chair matched the blue of his eyes.

Soon, Betsy from the fabric store stopped by with a quilted pillow.

"I made this for you," she said. "What a lovely chair. May I sit?" She carried it under a tree. Its buttons were square like the ones on her dress.

Before Abby could answer, Grace the librarian dropped by with a book titled *More Ways to Arrange Your Chairs in Your New Home.*

"What wonderful reading chairs you have." She pulled a red one next to Abby and sank into its soft cushions. The chair was even redder than Grace's hair.

Soon a new friend filled every chair. They
ate zucchini cake, sipped lemonade, and played
charades until the stars
came out.

When it was time to leave, Abby's new friends carried their chairs inside. Harold put his chair by Abby's painting table in the studio. Betsy placed her chair by Abby's sewing machine in the bedroom, and Grace set hers solidly beside the bookshelves in the den.

Soon a new friend filled every chair. They
ate zucchini cake, sipped lemonade, and played
charades until the stars
came out.

When it was time to leave, Abby's new friends carried their chairs inside. Harold put his chair by Abby's painting table in the studio. Betsy placed her chair by Abby's sewing machine in the bedroom, and Grace set hers solidly beside the bookshelves in the den.

Abby smiled. "My chairs look wonderful in my new home." Then she rushed to the door and waved. "Stop by again. Anytime!"